Echoes of Unrequited Love

Echoes of Unrequited Love

Dr. MizCyn King

authorHOUSE®

AuthorHouse™ LLC
1663 Liberty Drive
Bloomington, IN 47403
www.authorhouse.com
Phone: 1-800-839-8640

Published by AuthorHouse   02/12/2014

ISBN: 978-1-4918-5842-4 (sc)
ISBN: 978-1-4918-5841-7 (e)

Library of Congress Control Number: 2014901992

Table of Contents

DEDICATION

TO THE ONE I
UNCONDITIONALLY LOVE.
LOVING YOU INDIFFERENT
AS TO WHETHER IT WILL
EVER BE RETURNED.
AFTER ALL OVER TIME
UNREQUITED LOVE IS CAPABLE
OF FEEDING ON ITSELF
IT'S NO LESS BUT MORE.
YOU WILL STILL BE LOVED.

TO THOSE WHO HAVE LOVED
DARED TO LOVE
LIVED TO LOVE
THE HEROES THE HEROINES OF
THE AGES
LOVE ON
AND CONQUER.

I remain,
Indubitably Yours;
Dr. MizCyn King

NO LONGER

I am no longer seeking you
No longer yearning for you
No longer expecting you to be what you
cannot be
Affectionate
Caring
Concerned about and understanding me
I am on a voyage of self
A robin, a bluejay
Pecking feverishly to emerge
From the shell, the prison, the cage
That male chauvinism, male depersonalization
Entrapped me in.
Causing me to deny me
Lose me
Lie to me
About me
For lack of knowledge of who I am
Because I allowed myself
To be lost in you
Lost I am or was
Ah, but all is not lost

I've broken through the storm
I can glimpse the light of day
First a fleck
Now a glimmer
a full view
Of who I am
First my beak
It was shut by your silence
Now my wings
Tied to you in love, fluttering with emotion
That you resented
Now my feet
Ah, freedom.

ECHOES OF LOVE

My heart
Truly aching
Requesting
Your Love
Beneath the sweater's quaking
Are echoes of love
As tears
They stain my face
My cheeks
My neck
Trickle across the buttons
And wet my breasts
I ponder
I wonder
The complexities
Of these equivocal niceties
The chocolates
The bulbs
As I feel
My soul aching

Awaiting
A response
To these echoes of love.

<u>INDUBITABLY YOURS</u>

I long to love you
To be held
Caressed
Enveloped by you
Immersed in the warmth of your soft brown eyes
Haloed by your smile
Where I lose myself
Me
My anxieties
I long for your touch
The scintilation of the
Tips of the fine weave of your fingers
To reach you
To delve into you
To be one
I miss the sweet echo of your voice
That soothes
And smooths the rough edges
Ah, I yearn to smell you
Heaven scent
As we embrace

The vibrations of one ocean
Spanning to meet another
Tidal waves
If my love could transcend the miles
It would reach
Hold
But not possess
As two souls
Meet
Greet
Repeat
The language of love
Of a lifetime.
I look
I seek
I search
I've sought others
They are not you
No one else will do.

THE CORPORATE I

The corporate I
Incorporates you
In all I think
And say
And do.

RELATIONSHIPS

Sooth me
Move me
Choose me
Like you used to do
When we first met
I loved you
You loved me too.
Chase me
Embrace me
Caress me
Like you used to do
When you'd stroke my hair
Feathers in your fingers
Line my lips
Like notes from a violin
When we loved
Sweet innocence
Joy
Bliss
We had within.

LOST IN YOU

Drown me with your smile
Engulf me in your arms
Immerse me in your sweetness
Let me drip with your love.
Envelop me
Like tulip leaves
Surround the bulb
Love me
Laugh with me
Let me see the wrinkles on your brow
As you train
And show me how to tame
The raging fires of my love.

ETERNALLY YOURS

Like a morning cloud
Your love
It shines
Hovers
Over me.
Caught up
In the billows
Of eternity
Just you and me
Life
Carefree
It can
It shall
It must Forever be.

NATURE'S ANGLES

I see you
You see me
Through the gay artistry
Of the butterflies wings
As we mount
The sweet blossoms
Fragrant
Serene
We both grasp
The meaning
Of love.

HAZEL EYES

The stars glimmer brightly
From the fount of your eyes
They beckon
They delight me
To heights
High above.
They invite my soul
On a journey for two
My heart races
It ponders
As we cross life's seas
If there ever was
A love so sweet
As that
You've given me.

WILD FLOWERS

While I'm lost
In the mist
Of the green blades
Of grass
I'll struggle to hold
Grasp each moment
Make it last.
As I thrive
To be
A buttercup
Plucked up by your hand.
As you kneel
I bow and curtsey
To the fold of your hands.
O let me grow no longer
Nor tarry in dew
If it means
I must go on
Living
Growing
Without you.

BIRD'S NEST

Can you hear me
As I sing the melody of love
Of life that lasts forever
In treetops above
I am a swelling tide
Within the rustling leaves
Of a bird
Of a robin
Whose breast
Yearns for thee.

TAPESTRY

I am an oriental rug
Colors bright.
The hues
Waiting for your toeprints.
The softness
The touch of you.
Exotic
Vibrant
Like the peacocks tail
Feathers
Glorious Blooms
Cry out
In love.
We'll weather
The storms, yes, forever.
We'll weather
The tides breaking, we two, together.
We'll weather
The times apart, with cards or with
letters.
We'll mend them together

With seams
Of love
That weave the mystery of this oriental rug.

SAILING

A sailor
On the ebb tides of love
Marking my path
In the waves of your love.
No compass
No nautilus
No direction.
I man the helm
As I forge my way
Onward
In unchartered waters
'til my soul
Is made whole
With the prize.
Though I see
Nor sense
With my eyes
I will taste it
As the salt in the sea breeze
As I bow

And scrape before
You
Love scars on my knees.

ROLL WITH IT

Tumbleweed
Across the edges
Of your brow
Rocking
In the sands of time.
Enlarging
Ensnaring
Encompassing
Daring
To move forward
Adrift?
No
But with direction
left now
Then right
A swerve
But rolling
Swiftly
Idly?
No
Just wherever
You are

Where the winds of your will dictate.
Where love can be discovered anew.

CHEST

Blow off the dust
Open the lid
Fan the must
Of years gone by.
Of memories
Of laughter
Tears and joy
Go ahead
Pull out the drawer
A broken toy
That's me
Wind me up
You'll see
My drumsticks
Still pound a tune of love
Pull my string
Hear me sing
Of the times
I waited for you
To rediscover me
Roll me across the floor
Try again you'll see

Lost within these hallowed walls of cedar
A past love awaiting thee.

HARVESTING

Violets bloom
Over the years
Everytime the seed of your voice
Lingers in my ears.
The blossoms
Bend
Bow
In reverence
To the steady beat
The rythym
Of the promises of love
We've shared.
Do water me
With renewed vows
Of affection
Do shine on me
Like the sun
Love me
Plant new seeds
For perfection.

TWO STEPPIN'

Tap dance
On my heart
Make it start
Ticking
Hours
Minutes
Seconds
Left
Before
Love begins anew.
Seduce me
With your smile
Arrest my fears
The scars of years
Of time without love
And love without time.

ECSTATIC MOMENTS

Leaping
Spinning
Gazel-like
A top
Rotating
Pulsating
Exclaiming your love.
Don't stop.

DISTRACTED

Bouncing off
Landing on
The walls
You
Where life really matters.
Not amidst the chit and chatter
Where nothing
Means less
I seek your smile
Inviting
Defying
Time
All convention
Honorable mention
Just you
Where love
Seeks to love
Itself
To be
Recognized

For what it is
The serene essence
Of living.

BAR TALK

Fingers run
One
After
The other
Around the rim of the glass
As you plow
Furrows
Upon your forehead
Seeking words to employ
To say
The simple
Phrase
I love you.
On the rocks
Straight up
Emphatic
Sealed with chasers
Promises
Pregnant?
Empty?
Of time together again.

THE UNFAMILIAR

Test the waters
Don't give up
Don't give in
Take some lessons
Learn to swim
Don't linger at the side of the pool
Toe first
Then foot
Take a plunge
You might find love inside
Let the waters flow over
Your soul
Wash
Purge
Cleanse
Make you whole.

SPREAD YOUR WINGS

Express yourself
Be all that you can be
Live and let live
And you don't have to join the army
To be in love.
A flower glistening with dew
Yes, that can be you
A star shining brightly
Newfoundland
Find you
Ahoy there
A ship on a calm sea
Its you if you want it to be.

AFTER FIVE

Pausing
Lingering
Over the desktop
Peering within
Troubles
Overjoyed
I see your face.
But not you.
Fragments
Encased in glass
Polished frames
But not you.
Love unfurls
Sweat
Pounding beat
I love you
Heart swelling
Eyelids
Brim
Whelling
Overwhelmed

Love
Unexpressed
For you.

DE-SELFING

How can I
Think like a man
And yet emerge a woman.
Make a man's world mine
And maintain my femininity.
Be what you want
And yet still be and respect me?
Should I don a drab suit?
Wear a tie?
Low heeled shoes?
Bob my hair?
Observe the news?
But then what is left of me
Success, Love
With obscurity.

EASY

Its easy to say you love
With no commitment
Behind it.
Its easy to be in love
With no strings attached.
But is it love?
Or is love what you're afraid of?
Living it—no thanks
Its much easier just to say
I love you.
Please send
For
An interpreter
To review the line
I love you.

CAN YOUR LOVE

Can your love
Stand the test of time?
Can your love
Laugh away the wrinkles on
Your mind?
Can your love
Escape the trenches of hate?
Can your love be loved
Before its too late?
Can your love give
Without expecting a dividend?
Can your love lose
When you desparately wanted
To win?
Can your love Escape
The trenches of hate?
Can your love await
Love in return
If it comes
Too late?

SPELLBOUND

Overawed by your presence.
Overawed by your smile.
Overawed by your love.
Peeping over a cliff
Dangling from a tree
Let your love
Real love Capture me.
Overawed by the manner of your
dress.
Overawed by your sweet, gentle
caress.
Overawed by your walk.
The movement of your slacks
Your talk.
Overawed with suspense
At what you'll say to me.
Hanging from an airplane,
Suspended on a lift,
Dancing on the edge,
Teetering on a cliff.
Overawed.

Let your love
Real love
Rescue me.

MY BEST GAL

Lost her number
Got a dime?
Forgot her perfume
What a line.
Failed to call
Up too late.
Neglected to tell of the other date.
Meant to come
Misplaced your address.
Traffic lights
Left me confused, distressed.
Saw your best friend
Told her too
How I loved her
Not how I love you.
Let's take a raincheck
Your house or mine.
No!
Understanding ain't mellow.
It's just a line.

NO STEPKIDS

Heavenly Father
How many are there of us
Lost though in the house, in love?
Will someone sweep and search for us
Like the lost coin?
Will the hedges be searched
Will we be compelled to come in?
Will someone value us like
The pearl of great price
Or will our talents remain hidden, buried?
Will we continue to barter like the unjust stewards
Settling for less than what we are worth because of
The accident of birth, femininity
A nascent quality we dare not, cannot change?
Will someone graft us into the tree
Will we rise up and be the heiresses you made us
In love
In your image and likeness?

PLAYIN' THE FOOL

Friends
Side grins
Discourage
But I love you.
Misplaced
Out of grace
But I love you.
Irrational
Not fashionable
But I love you.
Friends
Side grins
Don't see
What you do
What you say
What you are
To me.
Why I love you?
But I love you.
That's a check you can cash!

FANTASY

A rolling stone gathers no moss
I'll wait until your edges square.
Everybody plays a fool
Then I'm a fool for you.
Love don't love nobody
Then
Nothing
Is what I am.
Without you
Without dreams
Soaring
Flying high
With you by my side.
A fantasy
Perhaps.
But dreams are what
Keeps love alive
And
I love you
I need to

Love you
To be me.
So, pardon my fantasy!

JUST LOVE

Planned
No
Designed
No
Schemed
No
Just is
Just spontaneous
Just love.
Satisfaction guaranteed
Love
No deposit no return.
Just love
Simple
Uncomplicated
Not sophisticated
Just love
Being itself
As only love can be.

FULFILLING

I can feed on you
Like bread
I can quench your thirst
Like wine
I can satisfy you
Like peace
I can draw you to me
Like hope
I can breathe new life in you
I'm love.
In love
With love
With you.
With the expression
Of caring
Of sharing
Of rejoicing
In love
With you
With me
With love.

DEMONSTRATIVE

I can be real
And love you too
It's no loss to me.
Love is giving
Love is sharing
The law of eternity.
I can be there
For you
Rather than on the run.
Yes, love requires
Desires
That we be one.
I can take time
To soothe your mind
To unruffle the pleated brow
I can entertain you
On the wings of love.
Come
Let me show you how.
So you were mistreated
Misread
Misled

By the love that you had before,
That was then
This is now
Love's descending Through
heaven's doors.
Come open up
Do let me in
Its cold without.
Inside
The warmth of love
Of friends.
Don't be dejected
Over the love you neglected or
The lover who rejected you.
Life's not yet over.
Don't play dead. Don't roll over.
Can't you hear love calling you.
My dear
You can begin anew.
Take a risk.
Risks you take.

If it's real love you want
Rather than fake.
Plant your seeds.
Water them too.
Add fertilizer
And prune.
And prune
Love's harvest will yield
Goods plenty
For you.
Love's calling you.
To love you less.
To love others too.
To grow
Expand
Be what it makes of you.
Love's calling
Over here Not
there.
Listen intently
You'll find
Love's found

Rather than left You
Behind. It's there
Look hard
Seek
Knock
You'll find
Love was there all of the time.
It's not hidden under a rock
It's not buried in the sea
It lies in the hearts
Of you
And of me.
Don't leave it there to rot
Bereft and alone.
Share it with others
You'll never be alone.
They seek love too
They have longings for you
They want the same love
That you want for you.

Don't be shy
Look inside
I'm ready for release
Love that is
Without Pride
LOVE.

LAPSING

Wait and see
If you wait for me.
But time waits for no man
As it spans eternity
Crooks the back
Bows the knee
But you speak
One day
We'll be free
Free?
Free without Love?
Without ties?
Without responsibility?
Without a mutual need?
You for me
And me for you
Then bind
Shackle
Imprison me
If it means
No love
If that's what it is to be free.

MYSTIC MOMENTS I

Mind still aglow
Thoughts aflame
Eyes sparkling
Reflecting
Your name
Etched in my brain
Written upon the face of my heart
Glowing embers
Brows knit
Pondering
The depths
Of love.
To fathom you
The deep
The why
When
you left
But failed to say
Goodbye.

(WITHDRAWAL)
MYSTIC MOMENTS II

You left before
You left ya' know.
Before the door
Opened
You were already gone.
Your scent
Drifted out in the night
Your hands
They left too
Recoiling
Despoiling
Eyes departed
Before we started
Cold
Arctic
Deep freezed
As your smile
Warm awhile
Left a chill on my spine.
You left
Withdrew
Taking all of me

My love
With the parts
Of you.

EPHEMERAL

Like a waif
Open windows
I sense you
I scent you
Ephemeral
Silken
Wondrous
I feel you.
Feel me
As you caress me
As you pass
With each breath of wind
I can taste
Your lips
On my face
Sweet chocolate.
I sense you
I scent you
As your eyes
First peer
Then pierce
Undress me

Then spade
Tunnel
Through the facade
The caverns
Passages
That lead
To the depths that lie within.
As love grows
It echoes.
Resounds.
First your head
Then your toes
It echoes
A symphony
In complete harmony
Of a warmth
That cold can never know
Love echoes.

LOVE STILL ECHOES "YOU"

Stay
Remain
Leave
Depart
Deport a part of me
From all of you
That's what it will be
Broken
Emasciated
Useless
Without you
You
Mystical
You
Wonderful
You
Glorious
You
Marvelous
You
Love still echoes
I Love YOU!!!

MIDDLE CLASS COMPULSION
(ON THE WILD)

<u>DEDICATION</u>

To all the black preppies, minorities and other nefarious elements *** who have braved the wilds of private schools, ivy league campuses, bars and accompaniments and the (chaos, con—fusion, delight, cravings, catastrophe, shock, boredom, success, failure—you designate) of corporate America. Welcome. To what?

*** While seated in the hallowed halls of a certain highly revered D.C. law school, a noted author and professor so referred to all non—whites as "nefarious elements." I was appalled. Nonetheless, you are welcome!!!

Dr. MizCyn King

INTRODUCTION

MIDDLE CLASS COMPULSION is the myth of the vivid and oft-times twisted imagination of a middle class professional. It is designed to depict the numerous internal conflicts that exist between the wretched and yet memorable ghetto like childhood, the toils of professionalism once attained, (though there was no "beginners course" in the home,) to maintain oneself "unstained and unspotted in the world," (which is a feat in itself since the big world is full of traps and snares and is basically perceived as amoral).

It is sad and yet amusing in it's description of the "tourist's" inner conflicts. They take on an added dimension when the tourist attempts to merge the multinational concepts of religion and worldliness, ie., attempts to cope with Christian morality and compete in a secular world. The tourist is torn between the desire to be successful and the need to be accepted by his/her peers as well as God. It appears that the twain shall n'er meet. In fact, whether the two worlds are compatible depends upon the individual. Here, I only seek to arouse your amusement at the futility of it all as our neo-professional, dubbed tourist, takes his/her first bath in the cesspools of accomplishment. There may be a touch of the familiar in it to you. Enjoy.

GENERATION GAP CHECKLIST

WANDER LUST

Gotta go
Gotta get it
Gotta have it
Gofer it
Gotta run
P D Q
Thoughts of you
Things is due
Gotta go.
Middle class compulsion is call—ing.

I. BETWIXT 'N' BETWEEN

Two worlds
Welcome
But you need
Welcome
But you don't have
Welcome
But you're overqualified
Welcome
Your faith in God must be denied
Not too welcome
After all.

II. BETWIXT 'N' BETWEEN

Two worlds
Miles apart
Each calling Welcome.
Your faith has been denied
Your virtue cast aside
Welcome.
Aye there's the rub
I will not come to you
I have not been subdued.
Your lies
They tantalize
The glitter
It mesmerized
I just realized
The cost would be too high.
Just won't fantasize
Unwelcome.

III. BETWIXT 'N' BETWEEN

I love you Lord
I must
To worship you
Torn within
Bandied about by sin
Won't you let me in
To worship you

Aye, the rub agin
It's not you
But it's me
Fighting against you
As Lord over me
Can I depart to be with T h e e?

I love you Lord
I must
To worship you.

GODS MANY

Served 'em all
Lust, greed
But I did not fall
You caught me.

Diamond rings
Jazzy things
Liz Claiborne
Rolex
Not far from you
O, have I strayed
You caught me.

Mercy dez payments
Mercy dez bills
Mercy dat education from on
the
hill.
Catholic school
Catholic clothes
Catholic hose
Mercy
You caught me.

It's still blinding
Not minding your ways
But minding mine
Doing my thing
Yet just doing time
Waiting for life
Life without time
You'll catch me.

<u>OPPRESSION</u>

Does not cease
When the oppressor ceases.
He leaves a residue
On the creases
Of your mind.

IMA

Ima
My, ma
Toiled all night
Toiled all day
So's us chillun could get away.
Ima
Worked and worked
Prayed and stayed
Moaned and groaned
Da chillun left home.
Ima
Dez back agin
Jes like you said
Eyes all red
Thought y'all was dead.
Ima
Chile come on in
Let's start over agin
Let go o'd'em sins.
Ima

It's night agin
Wondering where you been
Dey wouldn't let you in
Knows Ima

Unpack dem bags
Full of sad glad rags
Loss dat life o'which ye bragged
Says Ima.

So you'se back home
Get up off that phone
Don't want to be alone
O, they tell me of a home
Hey Ima.

<u>INERTIA</u>

The mind says go
The body says no
The feet say yes
But how will I dress
Then just sit and rest.

O, but morning has spoken
Like it usually does
Too late, the day is gone
Down, the sun
The mind says go
The body says no
Flip a coin.

GENERATION GAP CHECKLIST

A chasm, between,
my Soul and the Messiah
The mazzeroti
The Similac
The time you lost
that you'll Never get back
You played to win but when you didn't
Can't accept that Master payment.
Maybe its the rose you never got
Little things they say mean a lot.
Maybe its the curl that's in your hair
The frills, the thrills, lacy underwear
Ah, the laundry you never did
Open wide your heart and see
That something's between
my soul And the Messiah.

UNDERCOVER

Narcotics or
Narcissist
Drugs or paraphernalia
Check this, flashlight, neon light,
stop light
Just little o' me
Nothing more you see
Wanting to be
More than what you think of me
More than what you think you see
You see
The Savior gave me a job to do
And do it I will
No matter what you say, or think or feel.
I'm not a junkie
Nor am I a spy
Just the mote that's in your eye
Christian.
Everybody d'ats black don't do drugs

And drugs don't do everybody d'ats black.

ON LIBERTY

John Stuart Mill
Martin Luther
Or King, Jr.
Augustine or Plato or Nero
That is
Closer My God to thee.
With you is where
I want to be
It's the only place where I can be
Truly, truly, truly FREE.

UNLIMITED ACCESS
(Then Came You)

You met me there
Though I ran from You
You met me there.

You met me there
Though I sought You not
You met me there.

In a place where I thought I was free,
Never so much as acknowledged Thee
You met me there.

I shook and I trembled
When You called out my name
The fame and the fortune, the fluted frames
Why, they'll think that I'm lame
But You met me there.

The joy, the surprise
As the tears washed my eyes
You met me there.

No more guilt, no more shame
I will never be the same
Since You met me there.

YO CHRISTIAN COLLOQUY

Yo Christian
What's in it fo' me?
Heartache, misery and pain
Then why should I go
Ya know—I can't stand the raainn.

Yo Christian
It's my perogative
A free ride, talk some jive, man that's live.
Get sumbody else cause Lawd knows
I stands nothin' to gain.

Yo Christian
What ya gonna do fo' me
Nothin, just fussin, wanna be widya cousin
We're so sorry Charlie, gotta run
Driven me insane.

Yo Christian
Why don't they just let me live
All I hear is give
T'ain't caused nuddin' but pain?
Yo Christian.

BE DISCREET

Be discreet
Shaved my legs with neat
Put on happy feet
Don't dare hit the street.

Be discreet
Ya know yo'se is mine
Just lemme in sometime But
Be discreet.

Be discreet shrimp fettucini
Look real sweet
Love's ya dawlin'
Just Be discreet.

BLINDED BY PRIDE

Couldn't see inside
Just began to slide
Down that is
Down in the valley
The valley so low
Hang your head over
And hear the wind blow.
Couldn't see the darkness
Thought it was the light
Thirty-six big ones pearly and
white
Gleamed in the daytime
Blindin' 'em by night
Pearly whites
Blinded by pride
They said, it was my ego
I said dey was a lie
Blinded
O say can you see
Blinded
Lost and Found
That's me.

'IN

Usin'
And crusin'
Abusin'
And doin'
My thang
All that I want to do
Doin' it to me, Doin' it to you
Locked up, locked in
Silk and sin
Just coolin.'

STREET LIGHTS

Street lights
Finding me
Blinding me
Seducing me
To do, to have, delight
Have this dish I saw last night
And along came Sally
Straight up
In the alley
Language from the galley Of the
old sailor's home
Smelled like wine,
ugly to the bone
As she switched her behind
Tossed her head
Hair blood red
Parted her lips
Almost dropped dead
Only two oars in the ship
Almost got whipped
Sally was a trip.

JUST PASSIN' THRU

Stopped by along the way
Thought your man was cuttin' grass
But grass was smokin' him
Eyes was red and lights was dim
Didn't know what to make o' him
Cause you said he done got saved
Cause you said he mended his ways
Cause you said
Yes, you did, and I thank you.

Stopped by along the way
Thought you was havin' Bible class
Saw your shadow in the glass
Of that mirror, you was tuckin' away
Smelled somethin' burnin'
Head started churnin'
As you ducked in the kitchen
Yo old man was kickin'
'bout his coke you was lickin.'

Stopped by along the way
Thought your kids was 'way on vacation
My word what in tarnation
Is wrong with dat chile's eye
Said she fell while on the slide
At da 'musement park?

Stopped by along the way
Wit some good news
Good news you say
Of salvation, of Christ, the narrow way?
Luv ta hear ya
Hav ya set a spell
*Mutha just sent my check (Mutha =
welfare)
My section eight is due
My man's car note too
Ye just donno what I'm goin thru
Udderwise I'd luv to sit an chat wit
you.

SCHISM

Contention
Breeds in my heart
Dereliction of duty
Pushed us apart
Why talk to me
Yes,
Jesus loves me
The Bible tells me so.

Competition
Warring factions wage
Idolatry
Sets up the stage
O, they tell me of a home
O,they tell me it will be an uncloudy day.

Envy
Act I, Scene 2
Jealous of me
Whisper 'bout you
Lie about me
Please tell them

Lord, that I am yours
Why don't you just change me
Only way I can be
Completely yours.

BACKWARDS

What's ailin' you
Cheeks Red
Hair rinsed blue
Imitatin' American Flag?
Escapin' becomin' another old hag?
Where have all the flowers gone
The weeks, the days, the months
Shamed of gettin' old
Joie de vivre
Teeth laced with gold
Shamed of gettin' grey
Used to say it was wisdom
From the length of your days
Shamed of wrinkles
Porcelana, Atra and Dove
Where are the days, the days
Once blossomed with love.

FAMILY TREE

Still trying
Still reaching out
Still wanting them to care
Still wanting them to love me for me
Still yelling it's me over here
Still seeking some particle of understanding
Still wanting to be accepted
Still feeling sad, rejected
Still changing, roleplaying, modifying,
Meta morphizing
To be what they want me to be
"Gonna reach the unreachable star"

Spending my last dime
Giving all my time
Wondering why you don't see
That which is too clear to me
That I, an integral part of you
(And you, an integral part of me)

Am dying
Am winding down
Am failing to thrive
No water
No sunlight

No hope
No encouragement
No love
Still trying
To be what I think you expect of me
To make you proud
Still trying.
Even though I'm not allowed
To Belong . . .

BECOMING (TELEOS)

I will be a butterfly
A butterfly I will be
If I just don' let ya
Let ya hinder me
Cocooned for a long time
But I can hear on the inside
The harsh things you say of me
The doubts
The fears, the lies
The wasted years
The sadness
The songs
A child gone wrong
Just too headstrong
I can be a butterfly
A butterfly I will be
I'll flitter amongst the nectar,
The sweet blades of grass, the trees
My leaves will shimmer in the sunlight
As I drift along

I'll brighten up someone's darkened days
Become some discouraged child's song
I can be a butterfly
A butterfly I'll be
I'll glide through life in the daylight
Until some jar catches me.
I'll be that child's possession
Joy to him/her I'll be
I can be a butterfly
You just wait, you'll see.

PRESSED

Walk on me
I'll still get up
Trod on me
I won't be down
Go ahead, level me, pummel me, to the ground
God has given me
A spirit eternally free
No man can destroy me
I'm free, I'm free, you see
Afflict me
With your thorns and arrows
Pierce me in the side
Laugh and mock me as I grow
Lay my successes aside
Dress me in a crimson
robe
Let my blood run to the road
Yet no man can destroy me
I'm free,
I'm free you see
I've been chosen by Christ
I've got the victory.

MERRY CHRISTMAS UNBELIEVER

I will walk alone
If you won't walk with me
I'll tell the story of Jesus
Of Nazareth, of Gallilee
I'll witness of His love for you and me
How He is the only begotten Son,
The Father sent to set us free
I'll tell them about His simple birth
To parents of lowly means
Of a sky that opened up with stars
Of His plight (Herod's plot) and salvation dreams
Of how He laid in a manger
No crib for his bed
Of His death on the cross
His resurrection from the dead
His beautiful spirit
His lack of pride
When they spat in His face
When they pierced His side
He lifted up his voice
Abba, Father, He cried

Count not this sin against them
Lest they say I lied
Abba, Father, forgive them
For they know not what they do
They have not yet accepted
The gift sent from you.

<u>P</u> assive

   <u>M</u> ale

      <u>S</u>yndrome

TABLE OF CONTENTS

TITLE	PAGE

DEDICATION

ALL MALES, YOUNG & OLD
YOU KNOW WHO YOU
ARE!!!

P.S. M's, We love you!!!

PREFACE

I will posit the hypothesis that PMS may not be a biological or hormonal condition. Rather, it may stem from emotional deprivation—lack of nurturance of the female by the male.

You say ridiculous?! I say disprove it.

This work is a satire set in poetry on an arguably serious condition. It reflects the mood swings we women experience that the gynecologists call PMS. Yet, who will deny that PMS is identifiable only when there is a male-female confrontation brewing over a baseline issue of lack of attention? Think about it. The real issue is not the kids, the budget, his or her career and the conflicting schedules, the worn-out wardrobe, the need for new furniture, the grass or the other woman. The real battle is waged over one issue, the incessant cry "<u>WHAT HAVE YOU DONE FOR ME LATELY</u>?!!!!" The argument is over me, the woman, the better half, the significant other who is emotionally starved at any given point in time. The ME wants Q.T. that's all. She wants <u>Quality TIME</u> from her man. So what if it is during your football game?!

Ladies, I have dared to say to your man what you have refused to say out loud. Oh, yes, you may have said it but you cloaked it in sweet terms that allowed him to dismiss or ignore you. Or, you screamed so loud that he had you certified insane.

In any event, perhaps he will read this too. Perhaps he will begin to gain some true insights into those "rare, candid moments" when James Bonds' Octopussy or the deacon's daughter on AMEN turns into Fred Sanford's Esther or Julia Channing on Falcon Crest. For the Biblical enthusiast, when Ruth or Esther turn into Vashti.

If, on the other hand, he refuses to read it and dismisses it as the "insane babblings" of one of your twisted sisters, relax and enjoy it yourself. After all, it is you, isn't it?!

Enjoy,
Dr. MizCyn King

P. M. S.

<u>PASSIVE MALE SYNDROME</u>

T' ain't about blood
T' ain't about femininity
or it's impediments
Brain's not impaired
Nor is the heart
no dysfunction
Just blood
Just a curse
Could be worse
"But, you get so emotional"
"But, male, you play deaf and ignorant"
"I'm emotional all the time"
You deny yours
I own up to mine
Emotions
You don't hear til I scream
Just so happens
It's then I bleed
BUT

I still seek you
I still seek your attention
I still seek your affection
When I don't bleed
You just don't hear
Until I do
Bleed, that is . . .

Q.T. = QUALITY TIME

Him?
No stopping
Now
Or ever.
He's on the move
Yep!
Forgot the groove
Last night?
Lived it up?
Oh yeah!
How do you
Pray tell
MALE
I love you!!!
Scared away?
Let it ly
Another day
Shrug, laugh
Love you as you are?
Discomfort . . .

Mind set=
Who the hell
R U,
to demand
to be with
to be loved
by him?
Brain Dead or what?

CAPITALISTIC MALE

I'm a woman
Not a shoe
Put on and off
as suits you
I'm a woman.
Not a bed
where you lay
for rest
I'm a woman.
No request for your money
Require not
your keys
your car
your empathy
your credit
without you
they are nothing
because
I'm a woman.
need love
compassion
companionship

the same things I give
cause, I'm a woman.
Rise and shine
Male
I'm still here
And I'm a woman.

A SYMPATHETIC SPIRIT

My soul longs
Yea even yearns
For companionship.
For like mind
Like need
Like me
Better yet love
Seeking
Searching
Hoping
Anticipating
All is not lost
O say can you see
I'm in a crowd
Yet alone
Darkness shrouds, the friendship
Leaning over a funeral bier
The touch of your smile
Your smile
Or was it a laugh
Were you mocking
Laughing together with

Or at me
O the agony
Of searching
Seeking
A kindred spirit.

MUCH ADO 'BOUT NOTHIN'

Much ado 'bout nuthin'
When I say I need your time
Much ado 'bout nuthin'
When I say I love you
And await
And await
And await
The reaffirmation, reassurance
Of commitment
From you that you love me too.
It does not take that long to say.
It's not difficult to demonstrate.
But you're on the road you can't be late
For much ado 'bout nothing.

Much ado 'bout nuthin'
When I need your time
Much ado 'bout nuthin'
When I whimper and whine
Much ado 'bout nuthin'
I sit and cry and cry and cry

Much ado 'bout nuthin'
So nuthin' from nuthin' leaves
nuthin'
to much ado about.

MIGHTY MOUTH MURDERS

Your tongue
It cut deep
I wound
I bleed
I cry
I hurt
Yet you do not understand
You fail to comprehend
As you curse
It gets worse.
You dice
You slice
You sever
My flesh
From my bones
As you undress
And undo me
With the words
That you speak.
And you say you're the sheep
Of the Shepherd of Israel
Then why do you lie?

As you sit and watch me die
The last death.
From inside.

ELEVATOR SHOES

If I could turn back the hands of time
Wear yo shoes, make you wear mine
See if you'd take my perspective
As you took the directives
I take from you
See if you'd wear the smile
Turned upside down
As you ate what I dished out
If your bark would be as rough as your bite
If you'd wield the same clout
As you do
When you do
What you do
To me.

BAIT AND SWITCH

Luv ya!
Truly? Truly dear?
gettin quite lonely
you ain't here
see me
LONELY
you ain't here
I'm a woman
filled with fears
drawn to tears
need you HERE
Compete
on my feet
effete
ephemeral
amongst elite
all male
do tell
need you here
nothing like the real thing
no salt
need you

SHUGAH
No SUBSTITUTES WILL DO!!!

TOUCH ME NOTS

Touch me not
O gentle woman
Forsooth
I am too great
Yeah, you my number one woman
But
like the others you have to wait.
Only so much of me you see
to go around
I'se da only eligible bachelor d'ere is in town!

RATTLER TATTLER

I trusted you
On somber days
Your darkened ways
Betrayed me.
I trusted you
Eyes wet with dew
Lips
Ice morsels
Words
Igloo.
I trusted you
You betrayed me
I'll betray you.

COLLOQUY ON RECIPROCITY

Equal?
May not be
Matter not
To me?
Fair?
Who cares?!
Just demand
in fact, INSIST
Reciprocal right
to
Reciprocal love
and Affection!!!
But, you say
tired, woman
too tired
unless
I sense rejection in the air
suspect Jody on back stairs
then Awake!
all becomes fair.
no games
love and war

no mental scars
soaring, angry
sleep racked body
love you babe!

MS. FITTIN'

No can do
Live with you
Play content
Play the fool.
No can be
In reality
What you want
For me
What you want for you
No can do!

Something inside
Won't let me hide
My ambition.
I have a sense
Of my teleological condition.
I'm waiting to audition
For the leading role
The ultimate goal
To be me.
Played the game
Lived it too

Lived it via me
And via you.
Via everything you can name
Didn't fit
What a shame.

MS. CUSTER'S LAST STAND

No bananas today
tear down then
Empire State Building
must have
my way.
London Bridge? Bring it down!!!
Not a just lady
will rant
will rave
chase you
and away
til I get mine
way that is
"No" ain't in the vocabulary
"Wait" too pregnant to conceive
"Maybe"
Sorry
don't fulfill my needs
My soul says "Yes!"

NO SUBMISSION

WON'T be subdued
by fast strokes
WON'T be subdued
with threats or jokes
WON'T be subdued
No big bucks
No fine clothes
Saying brother
Spirit can't be broke
not breakin' my stride
not held
up
not laid
down
but movin
same pressures
same needs
same desires
same aspirations
same skills
same capabilities
as You

different sex
WON'T Be
SubDUED . . .

EXPLOITATION

Don't take me
Christianity
Femininity
for granted.
Beneath the calm veneer
Beneath serenity
it lies
frothing
brooding
Cauldron.
Don't tip it!
Fire
those that play
get burned.

Don't take me
Compassion
Love
for granted.
Beneath
Warm
Glowing embers

it lies
iceberg
mammoth
pushing
striving
your way
smooth but destructive
MAMA, tell him I don't play!!!

ODE TO THE SINGLE WOMAN

Pass me not
Sister! Hang on in there
O gentle man
Hear my
Sister! Hang on in there
Incessant cry
while on other sisters
Dear brother thou art falling
Sister! Hang on in there
Brother,
DO NOT PASS ME BY
Oh SISTER!!!
Settle not
for less?
than you've expressed
that you want him to be
Sister though you wait
Forever?!
Like eternity
Set up your standard
stick to it fast

Sister don't fall for some gigilo
who tickles your A__!!!
Wait til you git
what you want
Not wait
til you want what you git.
Sister!
Hang on in there.

ODE TO THE CHAUVINISTS

It aches
It pains
No sensitivity
To my pangs
Nor to me
You love me
Yeah, Yeah, Yeah
Reality
Don't bungle
This jungle (in you)
I'm in
You love me
Yeah, Yeah, Yeah
Pledge
Not your troth
but YOUR ALLEGIANCE
to me
Male Chauvinism
Male America.

FLEAS AND TICKS

Really tick me off guy
wonderin'
chile, why you do da thangs you do
actin' a fool
really tick me off though
seldom cry not cruel
subscribe Golden Rule
Iraq and I RAN
before you do unto me what I have
done unto you
really tick me off guy
cold, but true
no time for lovin' me
too busy lovin' you
really tick me off.

ULTERIOR MOTIVATION

WHAT Tis it
Honey
Makes ya move?
Makes ya groove?
Makes ya itch?
to be a _____!!!
What Tis it
Honey
Makes ya yearn?
to be so fast?
live in style?
live in class?
WHAT Tis it
Honey
Makes ya cry?
Makes ya lie?
Makes ya try?
though dissatisfied.
WHAT Tis it
Honey
Makes ya wheel?
Makes ya deal?

Makes ya strive?
Be for real
Honey
Incentive?
WHAT Tis it?

MATURATION

ANY THING
Leading to
constant inquiry
lacks perfection
lacks direction
cut from fabric
but patternless
no thread
useless
to mend
useless
just go
and grow
no seams to bust
no fear
just trust
in time
you'll be
YOU!!!

MOTHER WIT

Mama says:
Watch what ya marry!
Watch where you tarry!
Be it up
Be it down
It will carry you.
Don't wanna go alone.
Misery luvs company.
Don't mingle long with the wheat.
Stay way from the tare.
They put ya in a hole
Can't dig outta there.
Wheat? It'll hang with ya
til it find somethin' else.
Still end up
By yo' self.
Wheat sleep with ya
Don't wanna be seen with ya
Wheat lay with ya
But won't stay with ya
You ain't none o' theirs.

Give up on the fable
fortune and fame
eat sufficient food
fill your frame
stay clear of wheat
and tare
protect your good name
Mama says.

A MAZED RAT

How does it feel
to know
to realize
only people
ever loved or
ever chanced to love
or ever loved you
died
incapable of loving
no reason
no depth
no capacity to love
though you love
still longing
not met
still yearning
Maybe?
Too demanding?
Maybe?
Love too deeply?
Maybe?!
to love is to ly

exposed to hurt?
to love is to lose
to declare mortality
to self-destruct?
love synonymous with pain
love synonymous with suffering
love synonymous with hatred
thin line
to love is to live
to live is to love
is to long
Feel like a rat in a maze.

LORD, WHO?

Lord, who made these men
who prevaricate;
who procrastinate;
who predominate;
whom we emulate?
Lord, who made these men
who obfuscate;
who irritate;
who discriminate;
whom we adulate?
Lord, who made these men
who aggravate;
who dominate;
who adumbrate;
who cogitate;
who are always late;
who vacillate;
who equivocate;
whom we over rate?
LORD, WHO MADE THESE
MEN???!!!
"Excuse, me . . . ???"

Oops! Sorry.